I SURVIVED

THE GREAT MOLASSES FLOOD, 1919

I SURVIVED

THE DESTRUCTION OF POMPEII, AD 79

THE AMERICAN REVOLUTION, 1776

THE BATTLE OF GETTYSBURG, 1863

THE GREAT CHICAGO FIRE, 1871

THE CHILDREN'S BLIZZARD, 1888

THE SAN FRANCISCO EARTHQUAKE, 1906

THE SINKING OF THE *TITANIC*, 1912

THE SHARK ATTACKS OF 1916

THE *HINDENBURG* DISASTER, 1937

THE BOMBING OF PEARL HARBOR, 1941

THE NAZI INVASION, 1944

THE BATTLE OF D-DAY, 1944

THE ATTACK OF THE GRIZZLIES, 1967

THE ERUPTION OF MOUNT ST. HELENS, 1980

THE ATTACKS OF SEPTEMBER 11, 2001

HURRICANE KATRINA, 2005

THE JAPANESE TSUNAMI, 2011

THE JOPLIN TORNADO, 2011

I SURVIVED

THE GREAT MOLASSES FLOOD, 1919

by **Lauren Tarshis**

illustrated by **Scott Dawson**

Scholastic Press / New York

To all of you readers
who are new to America

B O

MOLASSES TANK

ELEVATED RAILWAY

COMMERCIAL STREET

CHARTER STREET

ON HARBOR

MAP ILLUSTRATION DETAIL

NORTH
END

BOSTON

CHAPTER 1

WEDNESDAY, JANUARY 15, 1919
AROUND 12:30 P.M.
THE NORTH END, BOSTON

Twelve-year-old Carmen Grasso was drowning.

She was caught in one of the deadliest disasters in the history of Boston. A gigantic wave had crashed in to the streets — a swirling, raging monster moving faster than a train. It turned buildings to rubble. It smashed wagons and motorcars and tossed trucks into the harbor.

1

Twenty-one people would soon be dead. Many more would be fighting for their lives.

This killer wave wasn't made of water. It didn't come from the sea. The monstrous wave was made of a thick brown syrup: molasses. For years, millions of gallons of sticky molasses had been stored in a building-sized metal tank. The hideous tank loomed over Carmen's neighborhood, blotting out the sun.

And in one ear-splitting moment, the molasses tank had exploded apart.

Carmen and her best friend, Tony, had watched in horror as the tank began to shake, as its rounded steel sides bulged in and out. The tank seemed to have come alive, as if it was boiling with fury, ready to destroy.

And then suddenly, thousands of the steel bolts that held the tank together let go.

Bang! Bang! Bang! Bang! Bang!

They blasted through the air like bullets fired from a machine gun. Seconds later, the metal tank blew apart completely. Jagged chunks of metal whirled through the air like knife-winged birds.

The molasses hovered in the air like a black, roiling cloud. And then, with a thundering crash, it hit the ground. Instantly, the streets became raging rivers filled with wreckage — chunks of wood and metal and glass, overturned motorcars and wagons.

Horses whinnied in fear.

Screams of terror rang out.

"Run!"

"Get out of the way!"

"Help me!"

Carmen ran for her life, Tony right behind her.

But the wave was moving too fast. Within seconds, the swirl of thick syrup had caught them. The molasses wrapped itself around Carmen's legs, like millions of powerful snakes dripping with slime. It rose up to her waist, to her chest.

She had to do something!

And then she saw it: a broken wagon, floating toward them. She and Tony both managed to climb on . . . until a huge hunk of metal from the tank rammed into the wagon.

Carmen tried to hold on as the wagon nearly flipped. But she slipped off and sank into the swirling flood of ooze.

"Carmen!" Tony screamed.

It was the last sound Carmen heard as the molasses rose up over her head and swallowed her whole.

CHAPTER 2

ALMOST FOUR MONTHS EARLIER
FRIDAY, SEPTEMBER 27, 1918
AROUND 3:30 P.M.
THE NORTH END, BOSTON

Carmen and her pal Tony were heading back from school, making their way through the noisy streets of their neighborhood, Boston's North End. Horse wagons clattered and squeaked, and motorcars honked. A young newsboy shouted out the front-page headline.

"DEADLY FLU HITS BOSTON!"

Usually Carmen and Tony would be talking and joking as they zigzagged their way through the packs of people that jammed the street. They would maybe stop at Ortelli's Bakery and see if they could sweet-talk Mrs. Ortelli into giving them a free creamy *cannoli* or crunchy *biscotti*. They always left empty-handed. But they kept trying, because anything was possible, right?

But today Tony was in a rotten mood. He walked glumly, skinny shoulders slumped. Carmen had been trying to cheer him up, but nothing was helping.

"He hates me," Tony moaned.

"He" was their teacher, Mr. Lawrence.

"No, he doesn't," Carmen said, for the hundredth time.

Mr. Lawrence was the nicest teacher they'd ever had. Over the summer, he'd come back from fighting in the Great War. He'd been badly hurt in a bomb attack, and couldn't go back into battle. So he came home and took a job as a teacher. He had a bad limp, but he acted like it didn't bother him.

"I'm stupid," Tony continued.

"No, you're not," Carmen said, rolling her eyes. How many times had she told him he just had to study harder — or maybe open a book for once?

That was why Tony flunked the first big math test of the year. Carmen knew it wasn't the F that upset him; he'd had plenty of those over the years. It was Mr. Lawrence's new idea to keep Tony in at recess so they could play some math games together. Carmen knew Mr. Lawrence was trying to help Tony.

Tony thought Mr. Lawrence was trying to torture him.

"That test was impossible!" Tony grumbled now, as they wove around a big pile of horse manure in the street.

"Well . . ." Carmen said.

She'd gotten 100, but she hadn't told Tony that.

She'd carefully folded the test and slipped it into the pages of the book Mr. Lawrence had lent to her, *The Wonderful Wizard of Oz*. The book was about a girl named Dorothy who gets sucked into a tornado and dropped down in a strange land called Oz.

Carmen couldn't wait to show the test to Papa.

He'd pin her perfect test up on the wall with all the others. Then he'd pat her cheek.

"This is why we came here to America," he'd say.

They'd come here four years ago, from a little village in Italy. The village was a beautiful place, where Mama's and Papa's families had lived for hundreds of years.

But in 1908, when Carmen was two, a powerful earthquake struck the south of Italy. Entire cities turned to dust in the quake. Minutes later, gigantic tidal waves roared across the land. More than 100,000 people were killed.

Including Mama, who was swept away when the sea rose up.

Carmen had only one memory of that terrible day — dim and hazy like a dream. She was clinging to Papa's back as the sea churned all around them.

"Hold on!" Papa had cried. "Hold on!"

Papa's voice had risen above the roaring waves, above the screams of the people all around them.

Carmen gripped *The Wonderful Wizard of Oz* harder as Tony kicked a rotten apple core into the gutter.

Papa never talked about the earthquake. But growing up in Italy, Carmen had heard the stories from her grandmother, Nonna. And reminders of the disaster were everywhere in their village — the crumbling church, the ruined school, the graveyard where Mama was buried.

Papa had wanted to stay in the village. But as the years crawled by, he realized there was no future there, especially for Carmen. The school never reopened, and most girls didn't go to school anyway. It was harder and harder for Papa to earn money as a farmer.

And that's why, when Carmen turned eight, she and Papa got onto a big ship and came here to America. They'd begged Nonna to come with them. But she'd refused.

"Someone needs to stay and watch over this place, *tesoro*," she'd told Carmen. That's what she called Carmen. Her treasure.

Carmen hated leaving Nonna. But she'd always been curious about that magical land across the Atlantic Ocean: *l'America*.

Carmen had imagined golden streets, skyscrapers topped with rubies, wide-open spaces where she and Papa would build their new life. Life would be much easier in *l'America*, she was sure.

Carmen smiled to herself now, remembering how shocked she was when she and Papa first arrived here, in the North End. She glanced around, flashing back to how all of this looked through her eight-year-old eyes.

The sagging buildings. The piles of trash. The dark alleys filled with howling dogs. She and Papa lived in an apartment so small there was barely enough room for the two of them — and the family of rats that refused to leave.

What was Papa thinking? she'd written to Nonna. *We made a big mistake coming here!*

Why would *anyone* want to live in *l'America*?

But Nonna wrote her back, telling her to be patient.

Trees don't grow overnight, she'd said.

Why was Nonna writing about trees? Carmen had wondered. There were hardly any trees in the North End anyway.

But soon Carmen understood what Nonna meant. It took time to get used to a new place. Like trees, she and Papa slowly grew into their new lives in the North End. She still missed Nonna, of course, more and more, even. And sometimes Carmen had to escape the crashing noises and crushing crowds. She'd find a quiet spot in her favorite park, close her eyes, and pretend she was back in the village.

She'd picture the Italian flag flapping in the town square, with its stripes and shield. Sometimes she could practically smell the sweet Italian breezes, a mix of lemons and flowers and the sea.

But the North End was her home now. She

loved school. There was always something new to see in this bustling city. And most of all, she loved their neighbors — Tony and his big, noisy family. They lived in the apartment right above them. They'd welcomed Carmen and Papa from the start. Most nights the delicious smells of Mrs. Grasso's cooking wafted under their door. And most nights Mrs. Grasso sent one of the kids down to invite her and Papa to join them for heaping plates of pasta or bowls of garlicky soup with *chi chi* beans.

Carmen glanced over at Tony now, smiling to herself. He was more like a brother than a best friend. She hated seeing him so sad!

But then she had an idea that would definitely cheer Tony up.

"Come on," she said, grabbing his arm. "I'll race you to the molasses tank!"

CHAPTER 3

Tony's face lit up as they took off running. Carmen knew he loved the taste of the thick, sticky syrup.

And he wasn't the only one. Kids from the neighborhood visited the tank all the time. The tank leaked. Molasses was always dripping down the sides, like ice cream melting down a cone. Kids would scoop the molasses into their mouths with their fingers, or turn sticks into molasses lollipops. Who needed to waste a penny at the candy store when you could get a taste of molasses for free?

"I thought you hated molasses," Tony said as they trotted along.

Carmen shrugged. "Maybe I'll take some to Rosie."

Rosie was a horse, an old mare who lived at the stable where Papa worked. Carmen liked to take her out for rides after school. They'd go to the park by the harbor. Rosie would nibble on the grass and Carmen would write letters to Nonna. Her grandmother loved hearing about all the people in the North End. But Tony was her favorite.

She called him *trottolino* — wild boy.

But today, Rosie and Nonna's letter would have to wait.

It took only a few minutes to get to the tank, which rose up over them like the mountains in Carmen's village back in Italy. Except the tree-covered mountains were beautiful. The tank was hideous — brown-painted steel covered with syrupy slime.

Tony slammed his hand onto the sticky tank. "I win!" he said gleefully.

Carmen grinned at her friend. She'd finally cheered him up! Nonna's voice echoed in her mind. *Ben fatto* — good job.

"Wow!" Tony said, pulling his hand away from the tank. His fingers dripped with syrup. "It's leaking like crazy!"

Tony was right about that. The tank always leaked a little. But today the goo was bleeding through the lines where the sheets of metal came together. Thick streams of molasses ran down the sides.

Tony stuck his finger into his mouth and closed his eyes.

"MMMMMMMmmmm," he said. "Tastes like Cracker Jacks."

Carmen dipped a finger into the syrup, then took a catlike lick.

"Blech!"

The molasses tasted sweet, but with a bitter,

black-licorice aftertaste. She shook her head and made a face.

Tony laughed. Then he smeared some molasses above his top lip, making a sticky brown mustache.

"Hello," he said, lowering his voice. "I'm Mr. Lawrence. Recess is now against the law!"

They both had a good laugh.

"Let's find some sticks," Tony said. He started walking around the tank, scanning the ground.

Carmen didn't need a stick — she'd had enough molasses, thanks. Plus, being this close to the tank gave her a queasy feeling. She tried not to look at the dead flies stuck in the goopy puddles on the ground. She wrinkled her nose as she breathed in the sickly-sweet smell. *Blech* was right. She stared at the tank, wondering why it leaked so much. Whoever built it did a bad job. And why did the molasses company have to put such a big tank right here? It blocked out the sun and ruined the views of the harbor.

And Carmen hated to think about what all that molasses was used for.

She'd heard Papa and his boss, Mr. Vita, talking about it at the stable a few years ago. They were in the little back office, playing cards. Carmen was brushing Rosie.

"They say it can hold more than two million gallons of molasses," Mr. Vita said.

Two million gallons? That sounded like enough to fill a big pond.

Papa whistled. "What do they do with it all?"

Carmen had been wondering the same thing. She knew some famous American foods had molasses in them, like baked beans and gingerbread. But two million gallons? That was a lot of gingerbread.

"It's used for bombs," Mr. Vita said.

"Bombs?" Papa said with surprise.

Carmen nearly dropped Rosie's brush.

Was Mr. Vita joking?

No. He explained that the molasses went to a factory where it was boiled down into something called industrial alcohol. Then it was used to make dynamite and bombs.

Strange, Carmen had thought. But then Rosie had snorted, impatient to get out for a walk. Carmen put the tank out of her mind. Back then, the molasses tank was just one of many strange things about America. Carmen had only just figured out that Red Sox weren't things you wore on your feet. And why did so many English words have sneaky letters that made no sounds?

The bombs didn't mean much to Carmen, either, back then. The Great War had just started, and America hadn't yet joined the fight against Germany.

But now, three years later, tens of thousands of American soldiers had been killed in brutal battles. She knew this war was bloodier than any before. There were new kinds of weapons. Like machine guns that fired hundreds of bullets a minute, and poisonous gas that burned soldiers' skin and lungs.

Carmen stepped back and stared at the ugly tank, as if she was seeing it for the first time.

She pictured Mr. Lawrence, limping through the classroom.

Suddenly this molasses didn't seem like any fun at all.

She looked at Tony, whose face was covered with goo. She couldn't help smiling a little.

"Hey," she said. "You done yet?"

"Just one more lick —" Tony started.

But he was cut off by a sound. A low, gurgling growl.

GRRR guh guh gug gug GRRR guh, guh, guh, guh . . .

CHAPTER 4

The growling noise got louder.

GRRR guh guh gug gug GRRR guh, guh, guh, guh . . .

"Is it dogs?" Tony asked nervously. He looked around, eyes wide.

Carmen's stomach tightened.

The North End was infested with vicious stray dogs that roamed in packs. They howled in alleys at night. And many of them had rabies. If you got bitten, you'd die a grisly death if you didn't get rabies shots stabbed right into your stomach.

The sound got even louder.

GRRR guh guh gug gug GRRR guh, guh, guh, guh . . .

The ground around the tank shook.

Carmen's heart pounded. Could it be an earthquake? She didn't think they had those in Boston. But what did she know?

She whirled around, ready to grab Tony and bolt. She imagined the North End crumbling apart, like her village back in Italy.

But the men working along the waterfront seemed to be doing what they always did. They were rolling their barrels and lugging their crates, talking and laughing.

"Look!" Tony cried.

Carmen followed Tony's gaze to the tank. The metal in front of them was vibrating, as if it was breathing.

Is . . . is there something in there? Carmen thought. Her heart skipped a beat. *What if it's a —*

But just as quickly as the noise started, it stopped.

The tank went still.

Carmen and Tony were so focused on the tank, they didn't hear the footsteps creeping up behind them.

"Hey! What do you think you're doing?" boomed a voice.

Carmen practically jumped out of her skin. She and Tony slowly turned around.

A big-bellied man with a greasy black beard and small, mean eyes stood over them. He was holding a huge club — and he looked like he was ready to crack some skulls.

"You're not allowed to be here," he growled. "This is private property!"

Carmen realized he must work for the company that owned the tank.

"Sorry," Carmen said, her voice shaking. "We were just worried. We . . . we heard noises coming from the tank."

The man shook his head and rolled his eyes, like she and Tony were scared little babies.

"So what?" he said. "It's always doing that. Molasses makes noise. It boils up sometimes."

He raised his club. "Now get out of here before I give you something to cry about!"

Carmen and Tony took off.

The stable was only a couple hundred yards away. They stopped to catch their breath behind a shed. Their eyes met — and they burst out laughing.

"I thought there was a monster inside the tank!" Tony cried.

He made a face and turned his sticky hands into claws.

"Rarrrrr!" he said. I'm the molasses monster! Slime shoots out of my eyes!

"Or maybe it was a shark!" Tony said, turning his

claws into a fin. "It sneaked onto the molasses ship and then wiggled through the pipe into the tank."

Carmen smiled. Tony really was smart. It was true that the molasses came to Boston on big ships. The ships traveled from Cuba and Puerto Rico — islands in the Caribbean. The molasses was pumped from the ships into the tank through a giant pipe.

Carmen caught her breath and brushed some dirt from her coat.

She didn't admit to Tony what she'd really thought when she heard those noises: that a person was trapped inside. What if a worker had fallen in and was drowning, being smothered by the disgusting, bitter goo?

Just the idea made her heart pound with horror.

But now she looked at Tony's grinning face and laughed.

Wait until Papa heard about this!

Carmen and Tony burst through the squeaking stable door.

Instantly, Carmen felt calmer as she breathed in the smell of hay and horses and heard the loud nicker of hello from Rosie. The mare was the only horse still at the stable at this time of day. The others were out pulling wagons back and forth across Boston. Rosie was too old to work anymore. But Mr. Vita loved her too much to sell her.

Rosie poked her white head over the door of her stall, flicking her ears and snorting softly. Carmen gave her a kiss on her nose. Tony rubbed her head — he loved her, too.

Rosie stuck out her long pink tongue and started licking Tony's fingers. Tony laughed.

"I think you like molasses even more than I do," he said to Rosie.

"Papa?" Carmen called. "We're here!"

Carmen expected to hear Papa's cheerful voice. He usually came running out from the back, to wrap her — and Tony — in a big hug.

But it wasn't Papa who appeared. Or Mr. Vita.

It was Tony's mother, Mrs. Grasso.

What was Mrs. Grasso doing here at the stable? Who was watching Tony's little sisters and his little brother, Frankie?

And then Carmen noticed the worried look on Mrs. Grasso's face.

More than worried.

Mrs. Grasso looked scared.

A stab of fear slashed through Carmen's chest. Had something happened to Tony's father? Had Frankie broken his arm again? Did one of the little girls get bitten by a rat?

But wait. Why was Mrs. Grasso looking at Carmen? Why did she have tears in her eyes?

"Carmen, *mia cara* . . ." — my dear.

She took Carmen's hands.

"I'm so sorry. But your papa is very sick."

CHAPTER 5

Carmen wiped away tears as she and Tony and Mrs. Grasso hurried through the streets. Mrs. Grasso had explained what happened — that Papa had become very ill around lunchtime. Mr. Vita took Papa home in a wagon.

"He's in bed now," Mrs. Grasso continued as they passed the bakery. "The doctor already came. He said your father has some new kind of flu."

The word *flu* made Carmen feel calmer. The flu wasn't really a killer, like typhoid or polio or rabies. Carmen had the flu just last year. She'd felt rotten and was in bed for days. But within a week she was back to herself.

Papa will be fine, Papa will be fine, Carmen repeated to herself as her boots clicked against the stone streets.

And looking around her, everything was the same as always. There were the little kids playing hide-and-seek between the pushcarts piled high with fruits and vegetables. There was Mrs. Ortelli through the window of the bakery, chatting with her customers. There was the gray cat sunning himself outside the tailor's shop, and the hams and sausages hanging in the butcher's window. There was a rat poking through a pile of trash.

And of course there was Tony, right next to her.

But then, when they stopped at the corner to wait to cross the street, Carmen caught sight of something else.

The newsboy, the one she and Tony had passed earlier. Carmen had barely listened to the headlines he'd been shouting out. But now Carmen slowed down and stared as the boy waved the afternoon paper at the people rushing by him. Suddenly his words seemed meant just for Carmen.

"DEADLY FLU HITS BOSTON!"

Carmen practically flew up the narrow staircase that led to their apartment. She rushed past Mr. Vita into the small bedroom she and Papa shared.

Another neighbor, Mrs. Perelli, was kneeling next to Papa's bed. But that man in the bed . . . that couldn't be Papa.

He looked like a shivering ghost, deathly pale, lips tinged blue. His teeth chattered, even though the bed was piled with blankets.

"Papa?" Carmen rasped, dropping down to her knees.

Papa's eyes fluttered open.

The ghostly mask fell away for a few seconds.

"Mia ragazza," he rasped. My girl.

Carmen sat down, blinking away tears, forcing a smile. She would cheer him up, just like she cheered up Tony.

"Papa," she said, her voice shaking. "I . . . I got another one hundred on my math test . . ."

But Papa's eyes were already closed again.

Carmen grabbed his hand — it was so hot! As if his blood was boiling, as if his bones were on fire.

She pulled a rickety chair over to the bed and sat down.

"I'm here, Papa," she said. "I'm here."

Hours passed, and the sun went down. Papa tossed and turned, muttering in his sleep.

And then came the cough, a hacking, wheezing cough like nothing Carmen had ever heard. It sounded like little bombs were exploding in Papa's lungs.

Mrs. Perelli and Mrs. Grasso sponged Papa's face and arms to cool him. They spooned medicine into his mouth.

But Papa's skin got hotter.

The cough got worse and worse.

Carmen sat in her chair, gripping Papa's hand.

Her mind kept drifting back to the flood after the earthquake, when Carmen clung to Papa's back as they were caught in the churning sea.

Nonna had told her the story so many times.

"I was up early that day," she always began, "because that naughty goat escaped again. I'd just reached the top of the hill when everything started to shake."

The earthquake lasted forty seconds but it felt like years, she said. When it was over, she raced down the hill to the house.

The roof had collapsed. But Mama, Papa, and Carmen made it out, and were safe.

"We thought the worst was over. But we were wrong."

The earthquake had caused the sea to rise up. Now tidal waves twenty feet tall slammed into the village.

"Your papa grabbed you and tried to run," Nonna continued. But nobody could outrun the sea.

Nonna always got a twinkle in her eye at this point. "The water was strong. But your papa was stronger."

He grabbed a shutter from a ruined house. He climbed up on it, and told Carmen to hold on to his back.

The water rose and rose.

They got separated from Nonna and Mama.

They floated on that shutter for hours.

And this was the part that had etched itself in Carmen's mind, especially the words Papa had called out to her over and over.

"Hold on," he'd said.

Now Carmen leaned into Papa, an inch away from his sweat-covered brow.

"Hold on, Papa," she whispered. "Please hold on."

She gripped his hand.

She held it tighter than she'd held on to Papa's back in the flood.

Tighter than anything she'd ever held in her life. She held on even after Papa stopped breathing.

Even after the doctor put the sheet over Papa's face.

Even after Papa's hand grew cold, and Carmen understood that some things get taken away, no matter how hard you try to hold on to them.

It wasn't until much later, when the sun came up, that Carmen finally let go.

CHAPTER 6

```
ALMOST FOUR MONTHS LATER
    JANUARY 15, 1919
       7:30 A.M.
```

Carmen was awake, but she kept her eyes squeezed shut.

The mornings were always the hardest. She finally eased her eyes open and took some deep breaths. She listened for Papa's voice in her mind like she did every morning.

Buongiorno, mia ragazza — Good morning, my girl.

"Good morning," Carmen whispered back.

"Hi, Carmie!" a little voice chirped.

Carmen looked down, and two sleepy brown eyes peeped up at her.

It was little Teresa, Tony's three-year-old sister.

"Go back to sleep," Carmen said with a smile. "It's still early."

Teresa flashed a gap-toothed grin and closed her eyes.

At the end of the bed, Tony's other little sister, Marie, was curled up under a tattered blanket. Carmen reached over and tucked her in tighter.

A snore rose up from the floor. That was Tony's six-year-old brother, Frankie. He was a skinny little bean. But he snored like a giant! He and Tony were asleep on a mattress tucked into the corner.

Across the room, the curtain that hid Mr. and

Mrs. Grasso's bed was already pulled open. Carmen could hear them talking in the kitchen.

This was Carmen's home now, the Grassos' two-room apartment. She'd been living here since the night after Papa died, when Mr. Grasso carried her upstairs and tucked her into bed with the two little girls. There were seven of them living here, crammed together like tomatoes in a jar. The noise was constant. The girls' giggles. Frankie's bouncing ball. Mr. Grasso's booming laugh.

And the fighting!

"Frankie bit me!"

"Marie wet the bed!"

"Teresa is eating a cockroach!"

No wonder Tony couldn't study!

But Carmen knew how lucky she was to be with the Grassos, who treated Carmen like family.

Carmen looked over at Tony, fast asleep with drool dripping out the corner of his mouth. He had hardly left Carmen's side since Papa died. He'd even started reading *The Wonderful Wizard of Oz* aloud at bedtime.

"It puts the girls to sleep," he said.

But Carmen had a feeling he was reading it for her. He somehow sensed that hearing about Dorothy made Carmen feel better, like she wasn't the only girl who sometimes felt completely lost.

Worse than lost. There were moments every day when Carmen's heart seemed to be crumbling apart, like the church tower in her village after the quake.

But then Tony would tell her one of his dumb jokes. Frankie would come racing over to show her a new baseball card. The girls would climb up onto her lap. Or Mrs. Grasso would ask her to stir the pot of tomato gravy. With all these kids, there was always work to be done. Carmen tried to help Mrs. Grasso out as much as she could.

Which was what she should be doing now, instead of lying here like a lump.

Carmen quickly got dressed. She stared out the window as she brushed the knots from her hair.

Of course, her gaze went straight to that ugly molasses tank rising up in the distance. It was impossible to look out the window and *not* see it. And now the tank would always remind Carmen of that terrible day that Papa got sick. She remembered those strange noises she and Tony had heard, how they'd run away in fear, and then fallen down laughing.

It amazed Carmen to think of how carefree she'd felt on that bright September day. She'd had no idea that Papa was sick. That the Spanish influenza had already sunk its fangs into Boston. That they would all soon find themselves caught in the middle of one of the deadliest disease outbreaks in history.

The epidemic spread through Boston and across the country — and the world. Tens of millions had died so far. Mr. Lawrence told them it was even more deadly than the Black Death, the plague that struck Europe during the time of the knights.

Here in Boston, hospitals ran out of beds. Schools and theaters and movie houses were shut down to slow the spread. But nothing helped. Bodies piled up in the streets. There weren't enough gravediggers to bury the hundreds dying each week.

Carmen wasn't the only kid at school who'd lost a parent. Some lost two, and brothers and sisters, too.

So much had changed since she and Tony stood together in the shadow of the molasses tank.

But that tank hadn't changed at all. It was still huge and ugly and leaking.

Carmen sat on the edge of the lumpy mattress to button up her brand-new boots. The Grassos had given them to her for Christmas. Her last boots were so small her toenails had turned black. Carmen stood up and wiggled her grateful toes. She figured she'd help Mrs. Grasso with breakfast and then head to school with Tony and Frankie.

She tiptoed toward the kitchen door. She could hear Mr. and Mrs. Grasso talking over their morning cups of espresso.

"Carmen's a gem," Mrs. Grasso was saying. "The kids adore her."

They were talking about her? Carmen crept closer.

"She sure is," Mr. Grasso agreed.

Carmen flushed, and smiled a little.

"When are we going to tell her?" Mr. Grasso said.

"The ship doesn't leave for another week," Mrs. Grasso answered. "No need to worry her about the voyage."

Carmen froze.

Ship? Worry?

"It's such a long journey," Mr. Grasso said. "It's going to be tough. Italy is very different from here."

The hairs on the back of Carmen's neck stood up.

"I know," Mrs. Grasso said. "But it's for the

best. Carmen and her grandmother will be together again."

Carmen stepped back. It was suddenly very hard to breathe.

The room started to spin as she understood what they were saying.

They were sending her back to Italy.

CHAPTER 7

Carmen stood there frozen, barely breathing.

Tony called over to her through a yawn.

"Hey, Carm. Are you pretending to be a statue or something?"

All the kids were awake now. Four sets of big Grasso eyes were on her.

"The Wicked Witch of the West cast a spell on her!" said Frankie.

The kids all giggled, and Carmen knew they expected her to join in.

But she couldn't laugh right now.

She pushed open the door to the kitchen — she had to get out of the apartment, before she burst into tears. She would go to the stable. Mr. Vita was in Connecticut, visiting his cousins. Carmen could get Rosie and take her to the park. She wouldn't have to talk to anyone.

She stumbled into the kitchen and headed straight for the coatrack. Mrs. Grasso stood up.

"Carmen? Do you feel all right?"

"Yes. But I'm . . . I'm going to school," Carmen lied, struggling to keep her voice steady. She threw on her coat. "Mr. Lawrence wanted some help —"

"So early?" Mrs. Grasso said. "It's barely seven."

But Carmen was already in the hallway, ignoring the voices calling after her.

She flew down the stairs and out the door onto the street.

Her mind was swirling.

How could they send her back?

This couldn't be Nonna's idea, could it? She and Carmen had been writing to each other nonstop, but Nonna hadn't written a word about that. The Grassos knew how much Carmen missed Nonna. Did they somehow think Carmen *wanted* to go back to Italy?

Somehow, she made it to the stable. She waved hello to Mr. Pallo, the cheery older man who was watching the horses while Mr. Vita was gone. She hurried to Rosie's stall. She didn't bother with a saddle, just climbed on up and clicked her tongue. Rosie knew that meant "go."

They headed toward the park by the harbor. Usually, the sound of Rosie's horseshoes on the cobblestones was soothing to Carmen. But today each footstep was a hammer pounding on her heart.

Clop, clop. She imagined herself saying goodbye to Mr. Vita.

Clop, clop. To Mrs. Grasso.

Clop, clop. To Tony.

She stroked Rosie's mane.

Who would ride her after Carmen left?

By the time they reached the park, Carmen's chest felt bruised.

She looked out at the ships, remembering when she and Papa first sailed into Boston Harbor. Papa was so excited!

"Anything is possible in America," Papa always said. "If you work hard, a person can be anything they want to be."

You couldn't be anything you wanted to be in southern Italy, though. Not unless you were already very rich. Papa had barely earned money as a farmer. All the men were farmers or fishermen; there were no other jobs. And girls? They got married and had babies.

Carmen wanted a family of her own one day.

But she didn't want that to be her only job.

Maybe she'd be a teacher, like Mr. Lawrence. Or a nurse, and help people who were sick. Or she could write a book, like *The Wonderful Wizard of Oz*.

She'd never do any of those things if she went back.

There wasn't even a school in her village.

Rosie came to a stop near the playground, as if she knew Carmen needed a break. Carmen slid down and buried herself in Rosie's mane, staring at her shiny new boots through the mare's soft white hair.

Suddenly, anger boiled up inside her.

She wasn't angry at the Grassos — not after everything they'd done for her. She was mad at herself. All this time she'd let herself feel a part of the Grasso family. But Mr. and Mrs. Grasso already had four kids. Mr. Grasso worked at construction sites, where he probably earned no more than thirty dollars a week.

Carmen should have eaten less! She should have tried to find a job in the factory, or as a maid for one of the rich families outside the North End. And she shouldn't have accepted these boots for Christmas.

Carmen kicked the dirt so hard that Rosie whinnied.

"Sorry, girl," Carmen said, giving Rosie a gentle stroke on the forehead.

Carmen paced back and forth, wrestling with the thoughts in her head.

School would start soon. But Carmen decided, for the first time ever, to play hooky. What did math or spelling matter now that she was going back to Italy? The only math she'd need there would be for counting goats and rows of tomato plants. She'd never speak English again.

Carmen stood there for what felt like hours, until she was so tired she had to sit down. She chose a spot under a tree and gazed out at the ships in the harbor. Again, she thought of Papa.

It had been Papa's dream to come to America.

But now Papa was gone — and so was the life they'd built.

Maybe the Grassos were right, Carmen realized.

Maybe it was time to go back to Italy. To her old life. To where she could be with Nonna.

Carmen leaned against the tree. She imagined her grandmother's arms around her. Then she closed her eyes and fell into a restless sleep.

CHAPTER 8

Carmen's eyes snapped open and she scrambled to her feet.

She thought she'd dozed off for a minute or two. But now the day was very bright. And warm. She unbuttoned her coat and looked around. Some men were on benches with open lunch pails.

It must be past noon!

Carmen couldn't believe she'd slept so long!

Everyone must be worried about her. She had to get back to the Grassos' apartment. Or maybe she should go to school. Maybe she should . . .

And then her insides turned to jelly.

Where was Rosie?

Carmen whirled around, but the horse was nowhere to be seen.

What a fool Carmen was! She hadn't tied Rosie up. And now . . .

What if the horse had wandered into the busy streets? She could get hit by a motorcar — that happened all the time.

Before Carmen knew it, she was running, screaming Rosie's name.

Carmen sprinted to the stable. She burst through the door and over to Rosie's stall.

But Rosie wasn't there.

"Think, Carmen, think," she said to herself as she ran back outside. Rosie was smart. Where would she go?

Carmen stopped and looked around. It was always so crowded down here by the water — even more packed than the streets up where Carmen lived. Men were everywhere. Trucks and wagons rumbled by.

Carmen was sprinting to a nearby shed when she noticed her eyes were watering. Her nose was burning, too. *Blech*. What was that sickly-sweet smell?

Molasses, she realized. The smell was thick in the air, worse than ever before. It even coated her throat. The molasses tank was just behind her. She turned around, and what she saw made her heart skip a beat.

"Rosie!"

The mare was standing at the tank, licking molasses off the sides.

Carmen almost cried with relief as she came up next to Rosie.

Smart horse! Carmen remembered how Rosie licked the molasses from Tony's fingers. She must have smelled the molasses in the air and followed it right to the tank.

"So you wanted a little snack?" Carmen said, patting Rosie's forehead.

The mare smacked her sticky lips. Her whiskers were dripping with goo.

"And I guess you're saving some for later," Carmen said. She grabbed a handkerchief from her pocket and started wiping Rosie's face.

That's when she heard it.

GRRR guh guh gug gug GRRR guh, guh, guh, guh . . .

Carmen ignored the strange growling sounds. It was just the molasses, boiling inside the tank. She knew that now.

And then Carmen heard a familiar voice.

"Carmen!"

It was Tony! He was running toward her from back near the stable.

Carmen swung herself up onto Rosie and clicked her tongue. They trotted over to meet Tony. His face was bright red, his hair damp with sweat.

"Where have you been?" he said, his voice cracking. "We've been searching everywhere!"

He looked so worried, and she could tell he'd been crying. Carmen reached down and grabbed his hand.

"I'm so sorry," she said. "I . . ."

But she didn't know what to say. She felt terrible for disappearing like she had. And now she wondered: Did Tony know about the plan to send her back to Italy? Did he realize that in a week, Carmen would be gone, and they'd never see each other again?

Just the idea of saying good-bye to Tony — to everyone — made her whole body shake.

But wait. It wasn't Carmen's body that was shaking. Or Rosie's.

It was the ground.

And this time she felt sure there was an earthquake. Carmen gripped Rosie's neck tighter, expecting the ground to split apart. The horse snorted and nervously stamped her feet.

"What's going on?" Tony said.

A man near them screamed out the answer, in a voice filled with panic.

"It's the tank!"

CHAPTER 9

GRRR guh guh gug gug GRRR guh, guh, guh, guh . . .

The noise got louder and louder, drowning out the honks and rattles echoing from busy Commercial Street.

But it wasn't the growling gurgles that sent stabs of fear through Carmen.

The entire tank was rocking back and forth. The rounded sides were bulging in and out.

The metal groaned and squeaked.

And then . . .

Bang! Bang! Bang! Bang! Bang!

Something small hit the ground, inches from Tony's boot.

Carmen stared. It was a tiny piece of metal, the size of Carmen's finger, covered with brown syrup.

"It's one of the bolts!" Carmen cried.

The bolts — rivets — that held the tank together. There were thousands of them.

And now all the rivets seemed to let go of the tank at once.

Bang! Bang! Bang! Bang! Bang!

They blasted through the air like bullets.

Bang, bang, bang, bang. Bang, bang, bang, bang.

Rosie whinnied.

They had to get away from here!

"Tony!" Carmen said quickly. She offered him her hand, to help him climb up onto Rosie with her.

"Get on. Let's go!"

But just then a rivet came whistling through the air. It hit Rosie in the neck. She let out a high-pitched, screeching cry, then reared up as blood spurted from the wound. Carmen fell off and hit the ground hard. And before she knew it, Rosie had taken off — without Carmen.

"Rosie!" Carmen screamed.

Tony was at her side in a flash, pulling her up.

"Are you okay? Are you hurt?"

But Carmen didn't have time to answer.

Kaboom!

The tank shattered apart. Jagged sheets of metal went whirling through the air.

As the tank collapsed, the molasses inside seemed to hover in the air for a split second — a massive roiling cloud. And then it crashed to the ground, a colossal, churning wave.

The gagging stench of molasses rushed up Carmen's nose and down her throat, deep into her guts. Screams of terror pounded in her ears, shouts in English and Italian.

"Help me!

"Run!"

"Get out of here!"

Carmen couldn't help looking back as she and Tony ran for their lives. She couldn't believe what she was seeing. The wave of molasses was at least twenty feet tall, and swirling and churning in every direction. With each passing second, it devoured more of the waterfront.

It smashed into buildings, tearing them to pieces. It picked up sheds and wagons, horses and men. The roar got louder as the wave filled with wreckage.

She and Tony ran as fast as they could. But the wave was faster.

Within seconds, it had caught them.

CHAPTER 10

Was this how Papa felt when the tidal wave swept up over their village? When the churning water grabbed him and Carmen and pulled them out to sea?

No, Carmen thought. Because this wave was nothing like water. It was thick and gooey. It felt alive as it rose up around her legs. Carmen had read about a kind of snake that wrapped itself around its prey, choking it to death. Now Carmen felt like a thousand snakes were wrapping themselves around her, trying to pull her down.

She and Tony locked eyes.

What should they do?

What *could* they do?

It became impossible to run. Each step was a battle through the thick slime. And with every blink, the molasses was rising higher.

To their waists. To their chests.

Carmen's clothes were soaked. The goo coated her skin. It was already hardening around her, trapping her inside a shell.

The molasses was up to her chin now. Globs splashed into her mouth, sickly sweet, sharp and bitter. It made her think of rot — of old garbage left out in the sun, buzzing with flies, crawling with rats.

Her stomach twisted. She was afraid she would be sick.

She and Tony looked desperately around. But everyone near them was struggling, too. There was nobody here to help them.

Carmen thought of Papa again, how he'd

found that old shutter to float on. That's what they needed — a piece of wreckage to keep them from sinking.

And just then Carmen saw it: something big, made of wood. It was part of a horse wagon.

"Tony! Grab that!" she screamed.

There was not a second to waste. It took all of Carmen's strength to propel herself forward through the muck. She pulled herself up on the wagon so half of her body was out of the molasses. Tony grabbed hold of the side. But before he could pull himself up, he lost his grip on the slime-covered wood.

Carmen clung to the wagon with one hand and she reached down with the other. She managed to grab Tony's arm, and with every last bit of strength she had, she yanked him up hard. He threw his arms over a wagon wheel, locking them together.

The wagon bobbed and wove in the churning molasses. Terrible sounds rose up around

them — cries of fear and moans of pain, the screeching of metal. Molasses coated Carmen's face, an itching, burning, dripping mask.

She and Tony huddled together, too terrified to talk.

All they could do was look around in horror.

Now Carmen knew how Dorothy felt when she fell out of that tornado and landed in the strange land of Oz.

Except that Oz was a magical land filled with bright colors and jeweled cities.

This strange place was a nightmare, a wasteland of rubble covered with brown slime. The destruction reminded Carmen of the pictures she'd seen in the newspapers of the battlefields of the Great War — the cities and forests of France and Belgium turned to charred ruins.

Wagons, motorcars, and parts of buildings swirled around them.

And people.

A man, his shoulder badly bloodied, clung to a barrel. Another man was thrashing wildly, trying to keep his head above the surface. A woman was facedown, not moving at all.

How many people were trapped in this flood? Dozens? Hundreds?

Was Tony's family safe? What about Mr. Lawrence and the kids at school?

And what about Rosie?

Carmen leaned harder against Tony.

And that's when he screamed.

"Watch out!"

From nowhere, a giant piece of the tank smacked into the wagon, nearly flipping it over. Tony managed to keep his grip. But Carmen slipped off.

"Carmen!"

Tony's voice was the last thing she heard as the molasses swallowed her up.

CHAPTER 11

Carmen desperately kicked her legs and spun her arms. She stretched out her neck to try to get her head back above the goo. But the molasses was like quicksand. The more she flailed, the deeper she sank. Beneath the surface, claws of metal raked into her leg, splitting open her flesh. She felt her blood spill out, gushing into the swirling river that was carrying her away.

It was no use struggling, she realized. The molasses was too strong, too powerful. How did she think she could fight back?

The force of the flood pushed her forward. She somersaulted in the muck. She gagged and coughed, struggling to breathe through her molasses-clogged nose and mouth.

No, she couldn't fight this. It was impossible.

Soon there was only darkness and pain.

And then a voice in her mind, just a whisper at first.

Hold on.

It got louder.

Hold on!

Papa? Was he here with her?

No. It was just his voice, calling to her. He was telling her what she needed to do. But this time Carmen was all alone in the raging flood. It would be up to her to keep herself afloat.

And she would not give up. Not without a fight.

She somehow managed to straighten her body. She let herself sink down until her feet touched the solid ground. Then she pushed off, propelling herself up through the goo. Her head broke through the surface. She managed to take a breath before she sank down again.

Hold on.

Down and up, down and up she went, over and over again.

The fourth time she came up, she managed to open her burning eyes for just a few seconds. Long enough to see an empty wooden crate floating by her. Long enough to reach out for it. To get her arms around it.

She held on.

Like she had before.

Like Papa had taught her.

Blood spilled from her leg.

Her heart slowed.

The world became blurred. Sounds faded.

But she didn't let go.

Not until the men found her washed up next to a smashed house, and pried her arms away.

They wiped the molasses from her nose and

lifted her up. Sirens wailed. Voices called to her. But Carmen felt very far away from the North End.

In Carmen's mind, she was with Papa.

And she didn't want to leave him.

This is the actual newspaper from the day after the molasses flood. Some information isn't correct because people were still learning details about this deadly disaster.

CHAPTER 12

```
THREE DAYS LATER
JANUARY 18, 1919
AROUND 7:00 A.M.
BOSTON CITY HOSPITAL
```

"Hello? Are you awake?"

Carmen's eyes opened.

A woman was holding her hand.

Was it Mrs. Grasso?

No. This woman was very young, with red hair and freckles. She was wearing a white cap.

73

A nurse, Carmen realized.

"Hello, darling," the nurse said, her Irish accent tickling Carmen's ears. "I knew you were waking up."

Carmen looked around.

A pink curtain surrounded her bed. She was in a hospital.

She tried to sit up, but her leg throbbed in pain. Carmen sucked in her breath.

"Don't fuss too much, love," the young nurse said. "You have quite a wound on your leg. Lost yourself quite a lot of blood. Doctors stitched you up, though. You'll be running around soon enough."

"How long have I been here?" Carmen asked. Her voice was scratchy.

The nurse fluffed Carmen's pillow and straightened her blanket.

"Three days."

Three days?

How was that possible?

Carmen lay back as the nurse took her pulse.

"You're in good shape," the nurse said, "compared to some of the others. Who would have ever thought that a molasses tank could explode like that? The whole waterfront is gone, you know. They're going to be cleaning up for months."

Carmen's mind was clearing; it was all slowly coming back to her.

The shattered tank. The raging river of molasses. The bodies floating by.

Carmen sat up and gasped.

"Tony!" she blurted out.

What had happened to Tony?

"Who?" the nurse said.

"My friend, my best friend."

Just then, someone called from the other side of the room.

"Nurse! We need you here!"

"Don't you worry, love," the nurse said to Carmen. "You rest now. I'll be back."

And she disappeared through the curtains, leaving Carmen all alone.

But she wasn't alone for long.

Carmen heard them before she saw them.

"I want to see her first!"

"No, me!"

"You pushed me!"

"Did not!"

A stampede of little footsteps clattered across the tile floor.

The curtains flew open.

And the three littlest Grasso kids swarmed around her bed.

They all stared at her, six enormous brown eyes.

Frankie broke out into a huge grin. He raised his hands up into the air.

"She's alive!" he bellowed.

Carmen laughed.

Mrs. Grasso came rushing after them, out of breath.

She took one look at Carmen and started

crying. But her face lit up with a smile even as the tears poured down.

Carmen held her breath, afraid to hope.

And then, seconds later, another face appeared.

Battered. Scraped.

Smiling.

Tony.

CHAPTER 13

Carmen was getting stronger. But doctors worried about the wound on her leg. They told her she needed to stay in the hospital at least another week. Carmen was tired of lying in bed. But at least she wasn't lonely.

Mrs. Grasso came every day with a feast of pasta or lasagna.

Mrs. Ortelli brought boxes of cream-filled *cannoli* and crunchy *biscotti* she shared with the nurses.

Frankie brought his baseball cards.

Teresa and Marie sat on Carmen's bed, braiding her hair over and over.

Mr. Lawrence brought books.

Carmen missed Mr. Vita. He still wasn't back from Connecticut. But Mr. Pallo stopped by one day.

"You have a visitor," Mr. Pallo said. "But she had to wait outside."

He helped Carmen out of bed, and to the window.

And there, tied up in front of the hospital, was Rosie.

"We found her near the stable," Mr. Pallo said. "Or what was left of it."

The stable had been destroyed, along with the fire department and almost every other building around that part of the waterfront. Carmen couldn't imagine how upset Mr. Vita would be. But at least his other horses were all safe; they'd been far from the North End when the flood happened. And now Carmen could see for herself that Rosie was all in one piece.

"The cut on her neck is healing up fine," Mr. Pallo said.

Carmen opened the window.

"It's good to see you, girl!" Carmen called out to Rosie, waving.

The horse's ears perked up. She let out a loud, happy whinny.

Tears sprang into Carmen's eyes, and not only from the relief of seeing Rosie unhurt.

Carmen realized she'd probably never ride Rosie again. Because not only would she be leaving the hospital soon. She'd also be leaving America. Nobody had mentioned that Carmen was going back to Italy. But someone would soon, Carmen was sure. Mrs. Grasso had probably already packed Carmen's clothes.

Carmen shut the window, forcing those

thoughts out of her mind. She had to focus on getting better right now.

Of all the people who came to visit, it was Tony she looked forward to seeing the most.

Tony told Carmen what happened after they were separated. His ride on the broken wagon had been short. He'd been swept out to Commercial Street, where the river of molasses became shallower and shallower. He'd sloshed his way out and wandered around in a daze.

"It was terrible," he told Carmen, his face darkening, his voice dropping down to a whisper.

The bodies — bent and broken, so covered with molasses that he couldn't tell if they were men or women. People crying in pain. Injured horses.

The mothers screaming for their children. Police everywhere.

Mrs. Grasso was already looking for him, searching frantically. She'd found him pretty quickly.

"And then we looked for you," Tony told Carmen now, his lip quivering.

Mr. Grasso had gone to the Haymarket Relief Station, a small hospital near the North End. That's where the dead were laid out.

Men who'd been working around the waterfront. A woman who lived in a house along Commercial Street. Two ten-year-old children who'd been near the tank.

But not Carmen.

More than 150 people had been hurt — carried away by the river of molasses, trapped in crushed buildings, struck by flying metal when the tank exploded. One man was blasted all the way into Boston Harbor. Injured people were in hospitals all across the city.

It was three days before Mr. Grasso finally found Carmen at Boston City Hospital in the South End.

Tony told Carmen something else that shocked her, what the molasses company was saying about why the tank broke apart.

"They say someone put a bomb in the tank."

Carmen had sat up in bed. "Those liars!" she'd exclaimed, her voice so furiously loud a nurse had peeked in to shush her.

But she couldn't believe it!

Everyone in the North End knew why the tank shattered — because it wasn't built right. Even little kids knew that. The tank had leaked from the moment it was built!

"Don't worry," Tony had said to her. "Nobody believes them."

Carmen could only hope Tony was right.

On her last night in the hospital, Carmen barely slept. Every time she drifted off, she'd fall into a nightmare. She kept reliving the moment when the wagon almost flipped, when she was drowning in the sticky darkness. When she heard Papa's voice calling to her.

And now Papa's voice echoed through her mind again.

Hold on. Hold on. Hold on.

Why was she still hearing these words? Carmen was safe now. Nothing was going to sweep her away.

But Papa's voice only got louder.

Hold on. Hold on.

What was Papa trying to tell her? What should she be holding on to now?

Sometime in the wee hours of the morning, Carmen got out of bed and limped over to the window. The moon was bright, and the flickering streetlights cast a glow on the city. She could almost see over to the North End.

Somewhere out there, the Grassos were curled up. Two girls under tattered covers. Two boys on the floor. Two parents in the bed across the room.

Her school was out there, too, waiting for the students to arrive the next morning. Mr. Lawrence had his lesson all planned out.

A warm feeling spread through her body. Because she suddenly knew what Papa was telling her: To hold on to their life here in *l'America*.

The life they had built together. The friends they had made. The school she loved so much.

She took a deep breath, lifting her chin.

"I hear you, Papa," she said.

Right then, she knew she would not — could not — go back to Italy.

If the Grassos needed help paying for her food and clothes, she'd figure out how to get a job. There would be people here to help her. The Grassos and Mr. Lawrence and their neighbors. Rosie, too.

It would be very hard, Carmen knew, to work and also go to school.

"Anything was possible" didn't mean everything would be easy.

But Carmen would hold on. No matter what.

CHAPTER 14

Carmen sat in a chair watching Mrs. Grasso cook up a storm. The kids were bouncing off the walls. The apartment was filled with delicious smells — garlic and tomatoes and milky melted cheese. Everyone was excited for the special dinner Mrs. Grasso was making in honor of Carmen leaving the hospital. Best of all, Mr. Vita was joining them, too; he was finally back from Connecticut. Mr. Grasso had gone to meet him at the train station.

"When is Mr. Vita coming with Carmen's present?" Frankie asked.

This was the third time today someone had mentioned a present for Carmen.

"Shhhh!" Tony said, slugging Frankie's arm. "The present is a surprise."

"You shhhhhh!" Frankie said, giving Tony a shove.

"I want a present!" Teresa whined.

"My present!" wailed Marie.

Mrs. Grasso looked up from her pot.

"Basta!" — enough! "Tony, please take everyone into the bedroom. Make sure the beds are made."

"But, Mama . . ."

"Go!" Mrs. Grasso said.

Tony looked at Carmen, who could only shrug helplessly. She wanted to help him with the kids. But the doctor had warned that Carmen had to rest her leg. Mrs. Grasso had ordered her to stay put in her chair.

Tony herded the kids into the bedroom. The door closed, and Mrs. Grasso looked up at Carmen with a relieved smile.

"Some peace!"

Carmen smiled back.

Tell her now, Carmen thought. They were finally alone. Now was her chance to tell Mrs. Grasso that she wasn't going back to Italy.

Carmen cleared her throat. She was afraid Mrs. Grasso would be mad, that she wouldn't understand. But Carmen still had to tell her.

"Mrs. Grasso," she said, "I need to talk to you . . ."

"Yes, dear," Mrs. Grasso said.

Carmen took a breath and blurted it out.

"I know about the plan. For me to go back to Italy."

Mrs. Grasso's eyes widened in surprise.

Carmen swallowed hard but didn't lose her nerve.

"I'm sorry but . . ." Carmen went on. "I over-heard you and Mr. Grasso talking about the ship. I know you want me to go back to Italy, to be with Nonna."

"Carmen . . ."

"I'm sorry but I've decided," Carmen said. She sat up taller in her chair. "I want to stay here."

There. Carmen had done it.

Mrs. Grasso rushed over. She bent down so she was eye to eye with Carmen.

"Carmen," she said. "We never said you were going back to Italy. You aren't getting on any ship."

"But I heard you say —"

Carmen's words were cut off by the sound of footsteps climbing the stairs and Mr. Grasso's booming voice. "We're back!"

The bedroom door burst open, and the kids spilled out.

Carmen and Mrs. Grasso would have to finish their talk some other time.

Tony rushed over to Carmen. He beamed at her. He looked like he was about to burst with excitement.

"I hear them!" Frankie cried.

The little girls were jumping up and down.

What was going on? Carmen knew the kids liked Mr. Vita. But you'd think Babe Ruth and the Red Sox were coming for dinner.

The apartment door swung open.

Mr. Grasso strode in, followed by Mr. Vita.

The room went strangely quiet. But the air seemed to crackle. Carmen noticed that nobody was looking at Mr. Vita. They were all looking at *her*.

And then someone else appeared in the doorway. A smiling gray-haired woman whose eyes blazed like candles.

Carmen blinked, sure she was dreaming.

But then before she even realized it, she'd

leaped out of the chair. She was rushing forward, hurt leg and all. Two strong arms came around her in a crushing hug.

It was Nonna.

"I missed you too much," Nonna said a few minutes later, when she and Carmen were alone in the bedroom, when they'd finally stopped

hugging and crying. "I wrote to Mrs. Grasso. Mr. Vita was kind enough to come to Italy, to help me make the journey."

So there *had* been a secret plan. Just not the one Carmen imagined.

"Did you come here to bring me home?" she asked Nonna, suddenly worried.

Nonna leaned forward, brushing the hair from Carmen's eyes. She shook her head.

"I think this is your home, *tesoro*," she said. "Your papa brought you here. And I know how sad the Grassos would be if you left. Especially that *trottolino* Tony."

Carmen looked at Nonna. Had it really been four years since they'd been together? How had Carmen lived without Nonna?

"Will you stay here with me?" Carmen asked. Anything was possible, right?

Nonna smiled. "For a while. We'll see how I like it."

Carmen hugged Nonna again. She breathed in Nonna's familiar smell — of lemons and flowers and the sea, of the village where Carmen was born. She felt a pang in her heart as she realized how much she'd missed Italy. Of course she wanted to go back there. Just not now. And not forever.

Could she and Nonna have two homes with an ocean in between?

She opened her mouth to ask. But there was pounding on the door, and restless, excited voices calling to them.

"Come on!"

"We're hungry!"

"I get to sit next to Nonna at dinner!"

"No, I do!"

Nonna stood up. "We better get out there," she said with a wink.

They walked through the door holding hands. Holding on tight.

There would be plenty of time for Nonna and Carmen to talk about what was ahead.

Right now, the table was set. Dinner was hot. And their family was waiting for them.

KEEP READING!

Turn the page to learn more about the
Great Boston Molasses Flood of 1919

Citizens investigate the aftermath of the flood while an ambulance stands by.

WRITING ABOUT THE MOLASSES FLOOD

Hello, readers,

It was one of you — an I Survived reader — who suggested that I write about the Boston Molasses Flood. (You readers give me so many great ideas!)

Like most people, I had never heard of this strange disaster. But of course I was curious. It seemed almost funny — a flood of sweet syrup! Some articles I read had silly titles, like "The Sticky Tsunami" and "The River of Goo."

But as I began researching, I quickly understood

that there wasn't anything funny about this deadly disaster. It was tragic, horrifying, and terribly sad. Twenty-one people lost their lives, including two children. Many of the approximately 150 people who were injured never fully recovered, and suffered for as long as they lived.

What made this event even more tragic was that it could have been prevented. This wasn't a natural disaster, like a tornado or a hurricane.

The molasses flood was a "human-made" disaster, caused by people who made bad decisions. That tank didn't just naturally sprout up in the middle of Boston. People *decided* to put it there.

It wasn't the tank's fault that it leaked. It was the fault of the company that owned the tank. They didn't test it properly after it was built, to make sure it was strong enough to hold more than two million gallons of molasses. They didn't listen to warnings that the tank was dangerous. They showed no care for the men and women and kids who lived and worked in the shadow of the tank.

And really, they are what this book is about. Like all the books in the I Survived series, this book is a work of historical fiction. That means all the facts are true (that's the "historical" part). The "fiction" part is the characters, who are from my imagination.

But these made-up characters are based on real men and women and kids who lived in Boston's North End at the time of the molasses flood, people I learned about in my research. They were mostly immigrants — people who had moved to America from other countries. The vast majority of those living in the North End at that time came from the southern part of Italy.

They left behind everything — and everyone — they knew. They crossed the ocean to start new lives in a strange land: America. Between 1880 and the 1920s, more than 23 million immigrants came to America. Of these, five million were from southern Italy.

Some of you reading this book are new

Italian and Irish immigrants wait to enter America, circa 1900.

immigrants. You know exactly what it's like to leave behind the country where you were born. To say good-bye to your home and friends and school. To move to a strange country where you have to learn a new language and customs, to make new friends and eat new foods.

And if you're not an immigrant yourself, chances are someone in your family was. Because unless you are a member of a Native American nation or tribe, someone in your family was born somewhere else. They came to America by ship or by plane or on foot, hoping to build a better life in America. If you are African American, your ancestors most likely didn't choose to come to America. They were captured in their homelands in Africa, brought to America in chains, and forced to work as slaves.

Do you know the story of how your family came to America? If you don't, ask your parents or another relative. I wish I knew more details about how my relatives first came to America. The story I know best is about my great-grandmother Elizabeth Yasnitz Rosen. She immigrated to America on her own in 1909, when she was thirteen. She came from Russia, where, because she was Jewish, she and her family faced prejudice and constant threats of violence.

Her journey to America was difficult. She arrived with no money, no English, no understanding of America. She lived with her older sister, Bessie, who had come a few years before.

My great-grandmother Elizabeth, on the day of her marriage to Nathan Rosen, in 1914

Their home was a two-room apartment in a crowded and dirty neighborhood, very similar to the one Carmen and Papa moved to in Boston's North End. Elizabeth went to work at a factory — at the age of thirteen. Her life in America was extremely difficult at first. But like Carmen, she slowly set down roots and came to love America.

If my great-grandmother hadn't found the courage to leave Russia and come to America, if she hadn't been welcomed here, I would not be alive today (and I would not be writing these words for you!).

Thank you for taking this trip back in time with me, and for inspiring me through the hard work of creating this book.

MORE FACTS

As always, I learned so much in my research for this book — so much that I couldn't fit everything into the story! Here are some interesting facts about the molasses flood and life in America in 1918–1919:

CLEANING UP AFTER THE MOLASSES FLOOD TOOK MONTHS

Within minutes of the disaster, the North End waterfront was swarming with police, firefighters,

A section of the tank after the flood

doctors, nurses, and other rescue workers. They worked around the clock searching for victims. They found them buried in the wreckage of buildings, trapped in molasses-flooded basements, and tangled up with twisted metal and wrecked railcars and wagons. What made the rescue efforts more difficult is that the molasses hardened. Rescuers had to use picks and chisels to free some of the bodies.

Firemen stand knee-deep in molasses

Cleaning up was an enormous challenge. Molasses was everywhere — in basements, pooled in the streets, hardened into a thick crust on the sidewalks. Plain water did little to wash it away. Finally, firefighters used a fireboat to spray millions of gallons of salt water from the harbor onto the streets and sidewalks. The salt loosened the molasses so workers could scrub it off.

A worker uses a torch to cut through part of the fallen tank.

The stink of molasses spread far from the North
End. It took about six months for the wreckage to
be cleared away, and for business at the North End
waterfront to get back to normal.

The elevated train tracks nearly collapsed when they were struck by a piece of the tank.

THE MOLASSES COMPANY REFUSED TO TAKE THE BLAME

From the start, it was obvious who caused this disaster: the company that owned the tank, United States Industrial Alcohol. They were in a rush to build the tank. They didn't build it correctly. They didn't test it properly after it was built. They ignored three years of leaks. One of their own workers, Isaac Gonzalez, was so worried about the tank that he had nightmares. He warned his bosses, but they shrugged off his warnings. Many people who lived and worked around the tank knew that it was dangerous, and that one day a disaster could happen.

But USIA refused to admit that the tank it owned was poorly built. Instead, they tried to convince people that someone blew up the tank on purpose. They insisted that someone had thrown dynamite into the tank, and that's why it exploded.

Few believed this. An engineer studied the wreckage of the tank. He determined that the steel the company used was not strong enough for a large tank. Also, there weren't enough rivets to hold the pieces of steel together. The company was supposed to test the tank before filling it with molasses. They should have filled it with water first, all the way to the top, to see if it leaked. But that would have taken time, and cost money. So USIA filled it with only a few inches of water, declared it safe, and then began using it to store molasses.

Three weeks after the flood, a judge for the city of Boston wrote a report. He rejected the idea that the tank had been bombed. The company's tank was shoddily built. That's why it broke apart and caused a deadly disaster.

USIA WAS PUNISHED FOR CAUSING THE FLOOD

Nobody from the company went to jail. But victims of the flood and their families got together and sued USIA. The legal case dragged on for six years. In the end, a judge decided that USIA should pay a total of $693,000 to the flood's victims. That might not sound like much. But today, that money would be worth about ten million dollars.

And it was an important victory for the innocent people hurt in the flood, and for those who lost fathers, mothers, children, and other loved ones. Because never before in America had a corporation been forced to pay victims when it caused a deadly disaster.

THE GREAT BOSTON MOLASSES FLOOD MADE US SAFER

Today, if you owned a company that wanted to build a giant tank, you would need to first get a permit from the city. Your plan would have to be approved by engineers. In other words, there are laws to make sure that nobody builds a tank — or a building, house, or factory — that isn't safe.

Many of those laws exist as a result of the molasses flood.

SCIENTISTS HAVE BEEN STUDYING THIS DISASTER FOR YEARS

It's been one hundred years since the molasses disaster. Since then, scientists have continued to investigate exactly why the tank collapsed when it did. They all agree the tank was poorly built, and that USIA was at fault.

But there's another reason why this tank was dangerous, and that's because of how molasses behaves when it's put inside a closed space. Molasses isn't like water and many other liquids that just sit in a tank. Molasses is alive with germs. These germs make the molasses bubble up. There's a scientific word for this: fermentation. Many people reported hearing strange gurgling noises coming from inside the tank when it was full. Employees who worked for the company knew that these noises meant that the molasses was fermenting. They knew that this could be dangerous, that the gases caused by fermentation can build up — and cause explosions. Fermentation put more strain on the poorly built tank and made a disaster even more likely. And yes, USIA should have known this, too.

MOLASSES USED TO BE MORE COMMON THAN REGULAR SUGAR

Molasses comes from the same plant that sugar comes from — sugarcane. Sugar is made through

Pieces of sugarcane

a complicated process of boiling sugarcane juice. Molasses is what's left over after making sugar.

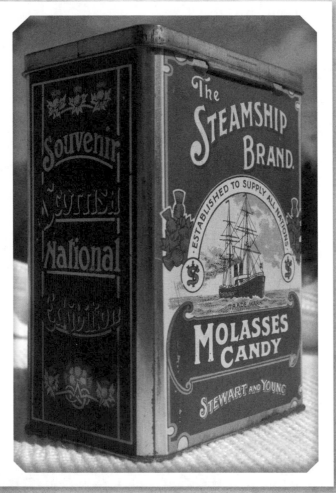

A tin of molasses candy, circa 1910

Today, you could live your whole life and never taste molasses. Mostly it's used to make old-fashioned recipes, like gingerbread and baked beans. (I have a dusty jar of molasses in the back of my kitchen cabinet that I haven't opened in years.)

But until the later 1800s, Americans used molasses by the gallon. Why? Because sugar was so expensive that most Americans only used it for very special occasions, like baking a birthday cake or sweetening the tea of an honored guest. Molasses was used to sweeten everything else.

But as sugar became cheaper, molasses was used less and less frequently in foods. And by the time the molasses tank was built, almost all the molasses brought to America was being used to make industrial alcohol, mostly for explosives and bombs being used on World War I battlefields.

IN 1919, AMERICA WAS CHANGING — FAST

At the time of the molasses flood, America was in the middle of a transformation. New inventions and technology were changing how people lived, worked, and traveled. New medicines and vaccines meant that people were living longer. More and

Men take a break from a road trip in their Buick motorcar in 1918.

more people were zooming around in motorcars; horses would soon mostly disappear from the streets of big cities and towns. Lightbulbs replaced candles and gas lamps, and made homes and streets brighter. There were new ways to have fun, like going to the movies and listening to the radio.

And there were more important changes happening, too, especially for women. For years, women had been fighting for equal rights — to be allowed

Women fighting for the right to vote were called suffragettes. These suffragettes are on their way to Boston, circa 1913.

to work in the same kinds of jobs as men, to open bank accounts, and, perhaps most important, to vote. In 1919 (later in the same year as the flood), they would finally win the right to vote in elections.

WORLD WAR I WAS THE DEADLIEST WAR THE WORLD HAD EVER KNOWN

Back then, World War I was called the Great War. It began in 1914. The causes of the war are complex; even today historians don't exactly agree why this long and bloody war started. But most historians put the blame on Germany's leaders, who wanted Germany to be more powerful. Whatever the cause, war broke out in July of 1914, with Germany and some other countries on one side battling the "Allied" forces of France, England, and Russia.

The biggest battles were in the forests and fields of France and Belgium.

Soon, tens of thousands of soldiers were dying every day in vicious battles. Soldiers used new kinds of weapons, including machine guns, more powerful cannons and bombs, and poison gas. Soldiers fought in trenches — long pits that protected them from some bullets, but also trapped them. Some soldiers not only had to fight in these muddy, rat-filled trenches. They had to live in them, for weeks or even months.

Most Americans wanted to stay out of this war. But in 1917, America joined forces with France, England, and Russia in the fight to defeat Germany. Over the next few months, nearly four million young American soldiers would fight in the war. More than 115,000 died and many more returned home with terrible wounds — legs and arms lost to bombs and bullets, lungs scarred by gas, dreams haunted by gruesome memories.

Worldwide, nearly forty million people died in World War I. That includes soldiers in battle and

American and French soldiers in a trench during World War I

regular people who died from war-related injuries and diseases that spread during the war.

The war finally ended on November 11, 1918, which became known as "Armistice Day." In America, we still celebrate that day as Veterans Day.

World War I was supposed to be "the war to end all wars." But tragically, that was not true. Just twenty years later, Germany's leader, Adolf

Hitler, started World War II and the Holocaust. That war was even more deadly. More than 73 million people around the world were killed.

THE SPANISH INFLUENZA SICKENED ONE-THIRD OF ALL PEOPLE IN THE WORLD

Scientists do not agree on exactly where and when the first cases of the Spanish influenza began. But the sickness did not begin in Spain. It was given that name because the king of Spain was one of the first famous people to die of the illness, in May of 1918.

Back then, few people imagined that this illness would soon spread across the world. But doctors were concerned. Because from the start, they understood that it was not an ordinary flu.

Many types of the flu are most dangerous for

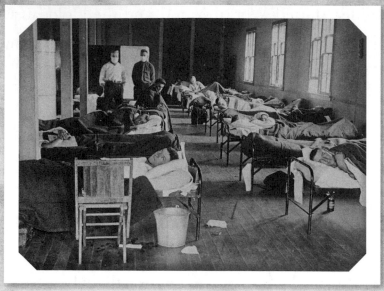

Spanish flu victims on the campus of Colorado Agricultural College in 1918

people who are very young, very old, or already weakened by another kind of illness. But the Spanish flu killed even the strongest young men (like Papa). The illness began with a headache and fever, and then often turned to deadly pneumonia that destroyed the lungs.

The first major US outbreak of Spanish influenza began outside Boston, on an army base. It quickly spread across the city — and the country.

Experts estimate that one-third of people in the world became infected with the flu; about fifty million died, including approximately 675,000 in the United States.

OLD-FASHIONED
GINGERBREAD

The molasses flood was such a sad story. But I wanted to end this book with some sweetness — a recipe for gingerbread cake. This is a delicious treat made with molasses. Kids like Carmen would have eaten gingerbread back in 1919. My four kids love it — and I think you might, too.

Ingredients
Butter or oil and flour for dusting the cake pan
½ cup unsalted butter
½ cup light brown sugar
1 cup molasses
1 large egg
2½ cups all-purpose flour
1½ teaspoons baking soda
2 teaspoons ground ginger
1 teaspoon cinnamon
½ teaspoon ground cloves
1 cup boiling water*

*Ask for an adult's help boiling the water.

Directions

1. Ask an adult to help you preheat the oven to 350 degrees.

2. Prepare a 9x9-inch cake pan: Grease the inside with butter or oil. Sprinkle on some flour. Tilt the pan so the flour sticks to the grease. Shake out any extra flour.

3. In a large bowl, beat the butter and sugar together with an electric mixer until light and creamy.

4. Add the molasses and egg and mix until smooth.

5. Add the flour, baking soda, ginger, cinnamon, and cloves and mix until smooth.

6. Ask an adult to help you carefully add the boiling water and mix until smooth.

7. Pour the batter into your prepared pan.

8. Ask an adult to help you put the pan in the oven. Bake 40-45 minutes or until a toothpick inserted in the center comes out without any crumbs on it.

9. Ask an adult to help you take the cake out of the oven. Allow the cake to cool before cutting it into squares.

FURTHER READING

Some books you can read about the molasses flood and that time in history:

The Great Molasses Flood, by Deborah Kops, Watertown, MA: Charlesbridge, 2012

Joshua's Song, by Joan Hiatt Harlow, New York, Simon & Schuster, 2001

Other I Survived books relating
to this topic and time:

I Survived True Stories: Five Epic Disasters includes the true story of a boy who survived the Boston molasses flood.

I Survived the Shark Attacks of 1916 takes place in New Jersey, a few years before the Boston molasses flood.

I Survived the Sinking of the Titanic, 1912 happens seven years before the molasses flood, and also features Italian immigrants.

SELECTED BIBLIOGRAPHY

"A Deadly Tsunami of Molasses in Boston's North End," by Julia Press, NPR, January 15, 2019

"Boston, Massachusetts," *American Influenza Epidemic of 1918-1919: A Digital Encyclopedia*, by University of Michigan Center for the History of Medicine and Michigan Publishing, University of Michigan Library

Dark Tide, by Stephen Puleo, Boston: Beacon Press, 2003

"How the Boston Molasses Flood Ushered in the Era of Modern Regulation," by Jared Keller, *Pacific Standard*, January 7, 2019

The Boston Italians, by Stephen Puleo, Boston: Beacon Press, 2007

The Great Influenza: The Story of the Deadliest Pandemic in Human History, by John M. Barry, New York: Penguin Group, 2004

The Long Way Home, by David Laskin, New York: HarperCollins, 2010

"The Life of American Workers," Monthly Labor Review, Bureau of Labor Statistics, February 2016

"The Science of the Great Molasses Flood," by Ferris Jabr, *Scientific American*, August 1, 2013

Can you survive another thrilling story based on true events?

Read on for a preview of

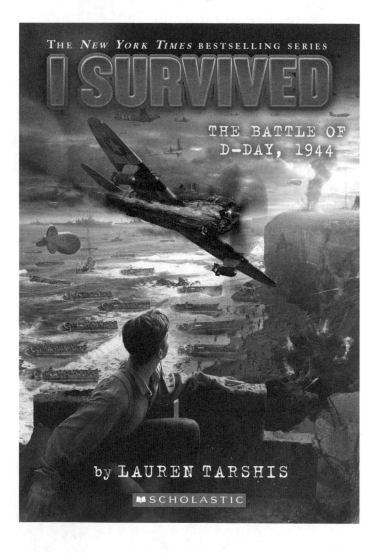

THE *NEW YORK TIMES* BESTSELLING SERIES

I SURVIVED

THE BATTLE OF D-DAY, 1944

by LAUREN TARSHIS

CHAPTER 1

Eleven-year-old Paul Colbert was running for his life.

It was D-Day, one of the bloodiest days of World War II. More than 150,000 soldiers from America, England, and Canada were invading France.

They had sailed across the sea on seven thousand ships, creeping through the dark of night.

Their mission: to free France from the brutal grip of Nazi Germany. It was time to crush the Nazis, and end the war.

In the minutes before the ships arrived, Paul was crouched on a cliff above the beach. He was trying to escape before the battle began. But now warplanes were zooming through the sky. And suddenly there was a shattering blast.

Kaboom!

Paul looked up in horror and saw that a plane was now in flames. And it was in a fiery death spiral, heading right for him.

Paul ran wildly as the burning plane fell from the sky. The air filled with the gagging stench of burning metal and melting rubber. The engine screamed and moaned. It sounded like a giant beast bellowing in pain.

No matter where Paul went, the dying plane seemed to be following him, like it wanted Paul to die, too.

And then, *smack!* Something hit Paul on the head. His skull seemed to explode in pain. Paul fell to the ground as the burning wreckage came crashing down.

For four long years, Paul had been praying for this day — for the war to end, for France to be finally free from the Nazis.

But now, it seemed, this day would be his last.

I SURVIVED

When disaster strikes, heroes are made.

Read th
bestsell
series
by Laur
Tarshis

SCHOLASTIC

ISURV

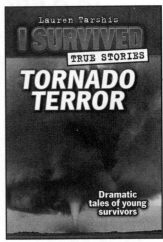